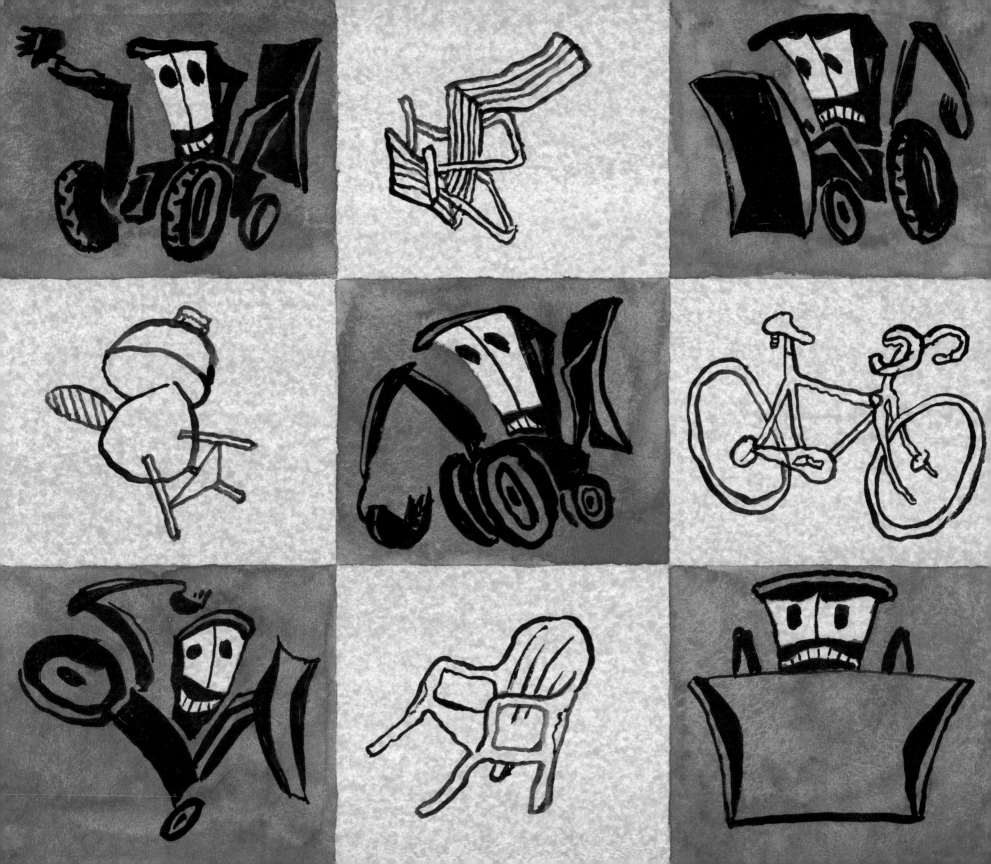

# I'M DIRTY!

## KATE & JIM McMULLAN

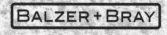

An Imprint of HarperCollinsPublishers

Balzer + Bray is an imprint of HarperCollins Publishers.

I'm Dirty! Text copyright © 2006 by Kate McMullan Illustrations copyright © 2006 by Jim McMullan  Printed in the United States of America.  All rights reserved. For information address HarperCollins
Children's Books, a division of HarperCollins Publishers, 195 Broadway, New York, NY 10007. www.harpercollinschildrens.com   Library of Congress Cataloging-in-Publication Data
McMullan, Kate.  I'm dirty! / Kate & Jim McMullan.— 1st ed.    p. cm.    Summary: A busy backhoe loader describes all the items it hauls off of a lot and all the fun it has getting dirty while
doing so.    ISBN 978-0-06-009293-1 (trade bdg.) — ISBN 978-0-06-009294-8 (lib. bdg.) — ISBN 978-0-06-009295-5 (pbk.)   [1. Backhoes—Fiction. 2. Cleanliness—Fiction.]  I. Title: I
am dirty!. II. McMullan, Jim, date  III. Title.   PZ7.M47879Ik 2006    2005017919  [E]—dc22  Typography by Neil Swaab      15  16  17  18   PC   20  19  18  17  16  15   ❖   First Edition

# For backhoe ace Michael Steiner

A great big load of thanks to the HarperCollins Crew:
Joanna Cotler, Justin Chanda, Alyson Day,
Neil Swaab, Ruiko Tokunaga, Karen Nagel, and Kathryn Silsand.
Also to Mindy Reyer, Jacqueline Moss, Peter Field,
and the kids at the Morris Center School;
Dan Steiger and Meridith Nadler;
Bill Villano at One Source Tools;
Antonio, Daphne, Gemma, and Paolo Caglioti;
and to my first-prize, cross-your-eyes Pippins,
Holly McGhee and Emily van Beek.

Who's got
a BOOM,
a dipper stick,
and a BUCKET
with a row of chompers?

ME!

And that's just my **REAR** end.

Up *FRONT,*

I've got **steel arms**, hydraulic rams, and a **specialized**, **maximized**, GIANT-SIZED **LOADER BUCKET.**

Flatbed truck?

*Get me to work.*

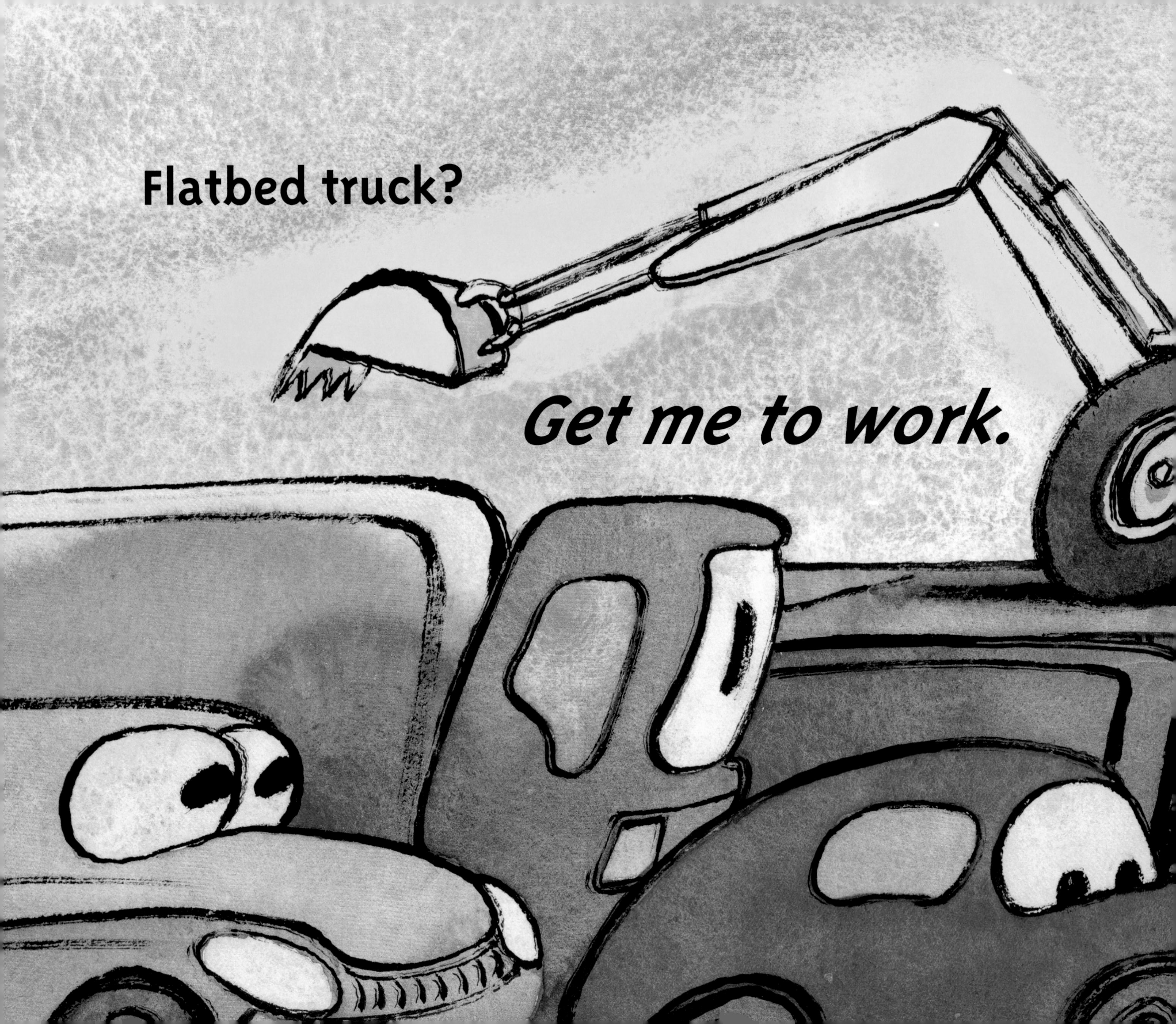

Backhoe Loader, reporting for duty.

Cleaning up this mess? Easy as pie.
Make that a MUD pie.

ABOUT-FACE!
Down the ramp . . .

$200 FINE FOR DUMPING

Counting down

**10** torn-up truck tires

**9** fractured fans

what I'm cleaning up:

**8** busted beach umbrellas

**7** loused-up lawn chairs

**5** burned-out barbecues

**6** broken bicycles

**4** cat-clawed couches

**2** tossed-out toilet seats

**1** wonky washing machine.

**3** scuffed-up signs

NO DUMPING

DON'T DUMP

$200 FINE FOR DUMPING

CLONK!

# Dumpster time . . .

On to the DIRTY part of the job.

Coming to take you out, Stumpie.

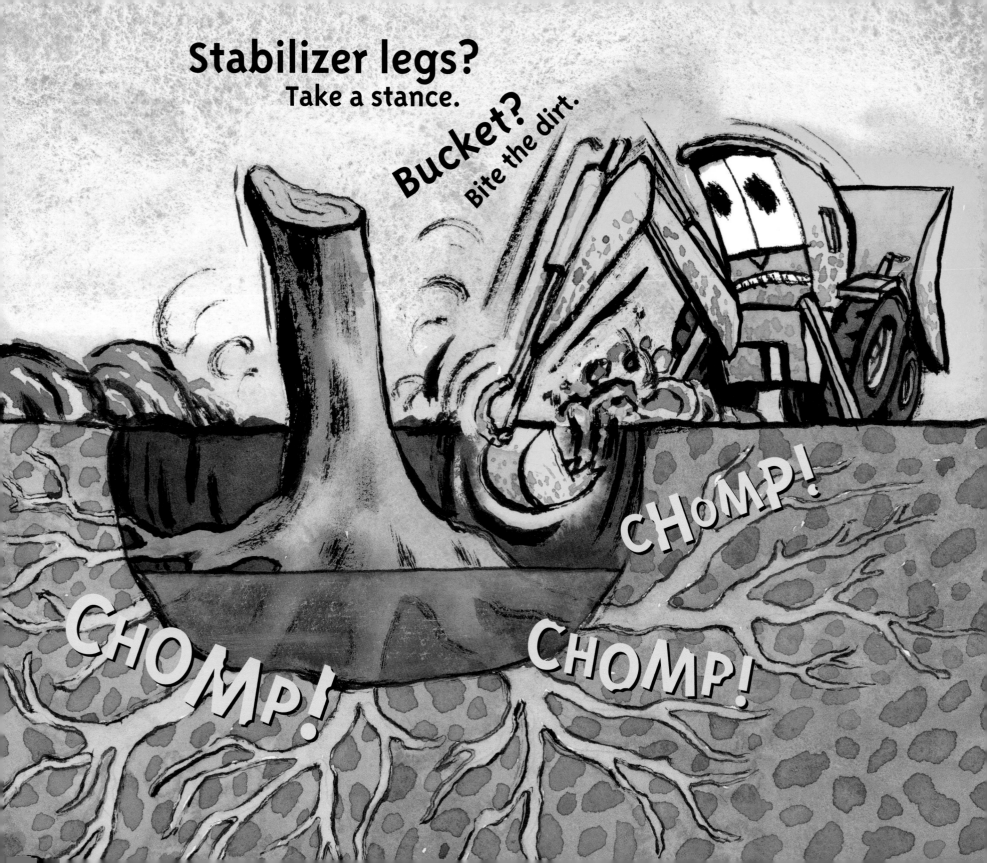

**Whew!** I need a **bath.**
Make that a **MUD** bath.

I like things **smooooooooth**,
so I shift it into **R**,
and back-drag the bucket over the dirt.

How's THAT for flat?

This lot's cleaned up.
And me?
I'm DIRTY.

Backhoe Loader, signing off.

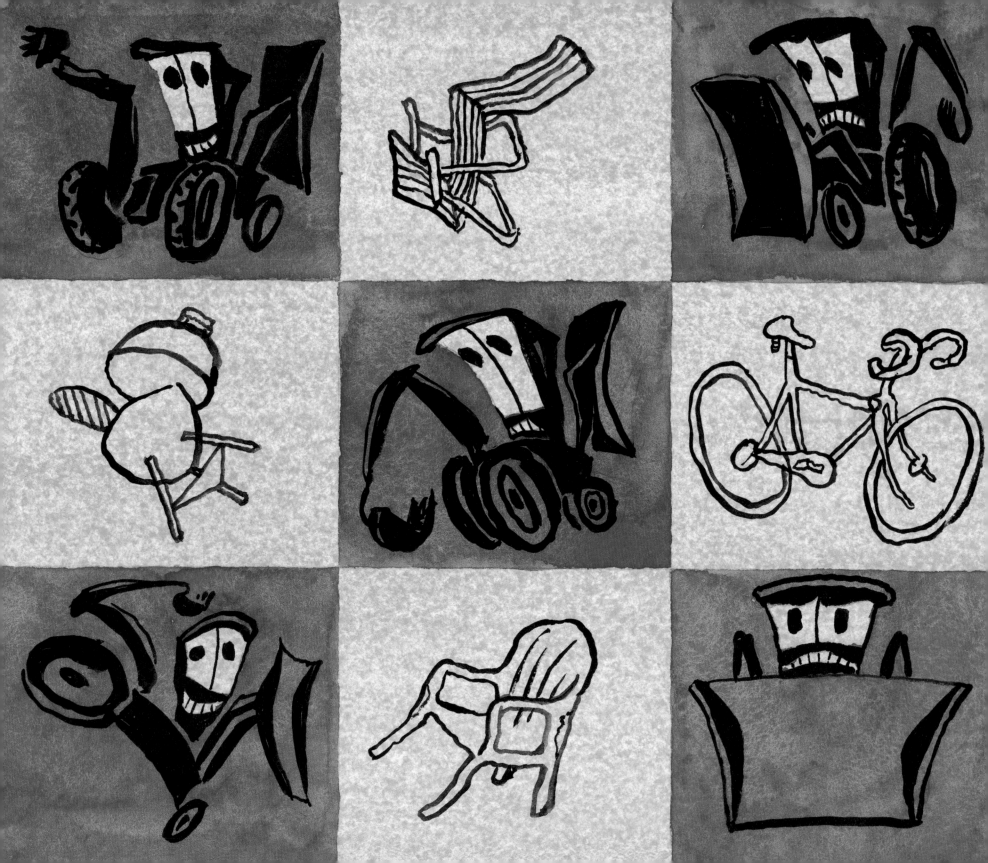